Fox woke up one evening with a rumbly, grumbly tummy.

"I am very hungry," he said to himself. "I will have to sniff out some food in town."

So Fox set off along the road, following his nose. First, he went to the bakery. He sniffed around outside, breathing in the yummy smell of crusty loaves, but no bread had been dropped there – not even a crumb!

Fox then went to the green where the market was held every morning. He put his nose to the ground and sniffed deeply. He could smell roast chicken, cheese, and apples. He searched and searched, but there was no food left anywhere on the floor.

"Not even a scrap for me," he wailed.

"I will go and look for food in the woods instead," he said to himself. "There is bound to be something there to eat."

So Fox set off for the forest, thinking about all of the yummy food he could get.

“There will be nuts, big mushrooms, and plump berries!” he said, drooling and licking his lips.

Fox looked under the trees, but all of the mushrooms had been eaten by slugs. Then he looked in the brambles, but all of the blackberries had been eaten by birds.

Fox's tummy rumbled loudly. Rumble, grumble, rumble, it went.

"There must be some nuts at least," grumbled Fox. But when he got to the hazel trees, all of the nuts were gone, too.

Fox squealed and his tummy growled.

“There is no food anywhere!” he wailed.

Fox looked all night, but he found no food. He crept back home to his den, tired and hungry. But then he saw a crow in an old tree. The crow had a big lump of cheese in her beak.

“A-ha!” said Fox to himself. “Food!”

Fox trotted up to the base of the tree and looked up at the crow.

“Good morning, my dear Crow,” he said.

But Crow did not reply.

“I see you have a big lump of cheese there,” Fox went on. “Could you perhaps give me just a little bit of it?”

Crow shook her head. Then Fox tried a different approach.

“I will flatter this bird into handing over that cheese,” he said to himself.

"What stunning feathers you have, and what elegant black wings!" said Fox to Crow. "Why, you are the best-looking bird I have seen tonight."

Fox charmed Crow as best he could, but she still held on tightly to the cheese in her beak.

Fox did not give up.

"I bet you can sing splendidly. All birds sing splendidly. If you could sing just one note, I would call you the Queen of Birds!"

Crow very much wanted to be called the Queen of Birds. She wanted it so much that she forgot to hold onto her cheese. She opened her beak wide, and let out a loud squawk.

"Caw-caw," she squawked.

With that, the big lump of cheese fell out of her beak, and straight into Fox's wide open mouth.

"Yum, yum, yum!" said Fox, delightedly as he gobbled it up.

"My cheese!" wailed Crow.

But Fox just licked his lips.

As the Sun rose, Fox trotted off happily to his den. His tummy was no longer rumbling.

"I will sleep well today," he said to himself.